Hooray for You!

A Celebration of "You-ness"

By Marianne Richmond

Hooray for You!

LCCN 2001035347

Marianne Richmond Studios, Inc.
420 N. 5th Street, Suite 840
Minneapolis, MN 55401
www.mariannerichmond.com

ISBN 10: 0-9763101-8-X
ISBN 13: 978-0-9763101-8-1

Illustrations by Marianne Richmond

Book design by Sara Dare Biscan

Printed in USA

Fifth Printing

Also available from author & illustrator
Marianne Richmond:

The Gift of an Angel
The Gift of a Memory
The Gifts of Being Grand
I Love You So...
Dear Daughter
Dear Son
My Shoes Take Me Where I Want to Go
Fish Kisses and Gorilla Hugs
Dear Granddaughter
Dear Grandson

Plus, she now offers the *simply said...* and *smartly said...* mini book titles
for all occasions.

To learn more about Marianne's products,
please visit
www.mariannerichmond.com

Hooray for You!

is dedicated to

Cole James, Adam Jon, Julia Rose, and Will David
whose you-ness I adore.—MR

For quite a long time, the world saved a place.

Millions were born, yet none filled your space...

Until the second of a minute of one special day,

you took your first breath

and the world said

Hooray!

Perfectly timed. Not one minute more.

You suddenly were where you were not before.

You

But planning preceded your earthly debut

as all was completed in the you-ness of you.

Great Job!

"You-ness?" you ask. Quite hard to describe,

it's your style of being, your rhythm or vibe.

It's the grand sum of you that sets you apart.

Your body and brains plus your spirit and heart.

"Okay..." you might think,
"but I'm not sure I see
why the big fuss
and hooray about me."

Then get set to enjoy
the big celebration
of the you-ness of you,
a remarkable creation!

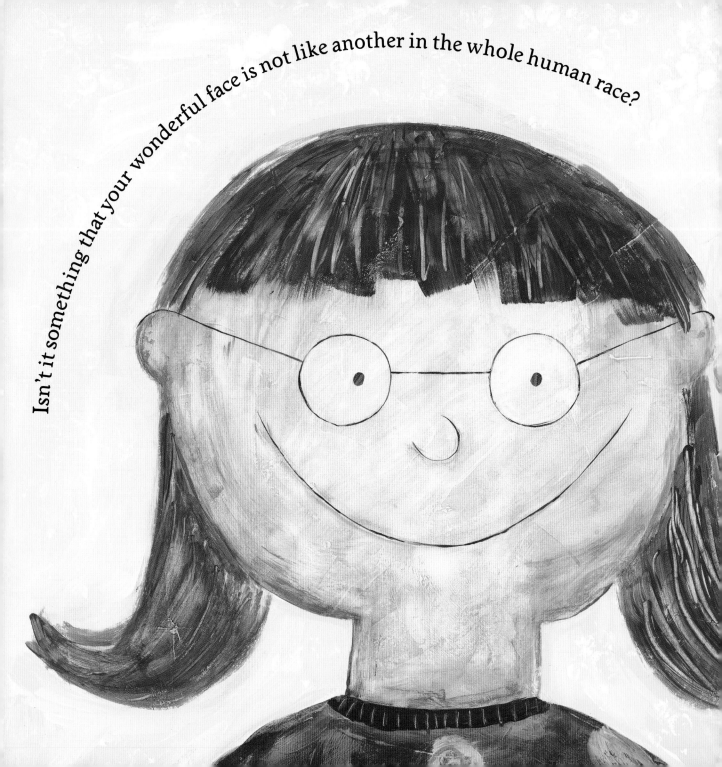

Isn't it something that your wonderful face is not like another in the whole human race?

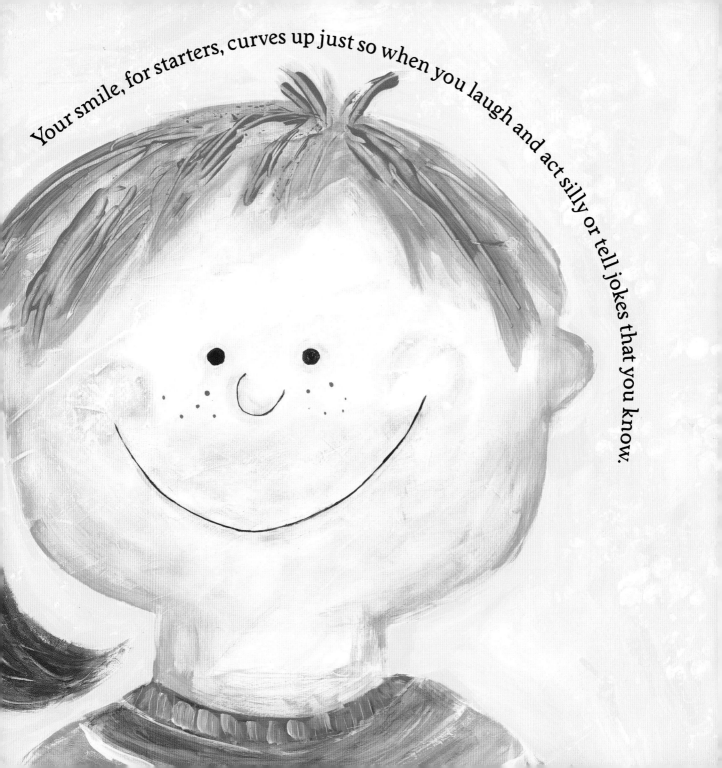

Your smile, for starters, curves up just so when you laugh and act silly or tell jokes that you know.

The body you live in
can jump, dance and play
with custom built parts
to move your own way.

Even your hair be it black, brown or red

does its own thing on top of your head.

And your certain good looks are just one teensy part

of the you-ness galore of your mind and your heart.

This is the essence of what you're about,

the true who of you within and throughout.

For instance, the way your brain likes to think.

"It just happens," you say, like a sneeze or a blink.

Automatic, for sure, but predictable not,

for no other has your process of thought.

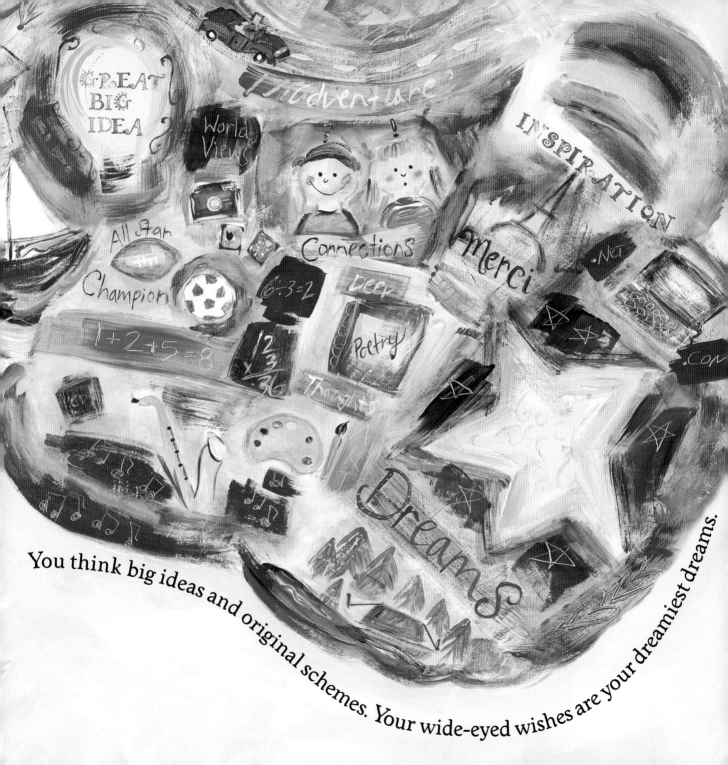

You think big ideas and original schemes. Your wide-eyed wishes are your dreamiest dreams.

And your feelings deep down are colorful creations,
a kaleidoscope of moods and emotional sensations.

Who else can know your kind of glad,

silly, excited, grumpy or sad?

There are foods you find yummy. A favorite color or two.

Things you don't like, but more that you do!

And the cool thing that's true

is how you can grow

when there's thinking to change

or new stuff to know.

You're perfect as you, but my friend, you will see

days when delighted is not what you'll be.

You might even think, "I'd sure wish to be

like him, her or them. Any person but me!"

Gloom

Toothpaste

Then stop that at once.

Put gloom on the shelf.

Say, "Good-bye doubt"

and "HOORAY SELF!"

The Big Catch

If people compare
you with another
like a mother or sister
or uncle or brother

Family Reunion

To them you can say for certain indeed,

"I'm completely for sure ME guaranteed!"

Me!

Yes, from head to toe tip, you're truly original,

a creation-in-progress, a distinct individual.

Look the world over, and you'll never find

a duplicate of you-ness that's your one-of-a-kind!

A gifted author and illustrator, Marianne Richmond
lives in Minneapolis, Minnesota with her husband,
Jim, and their four children.

The idea for **Hooray for You!** came about as Marianne considered why
we cherish certain people in our lives. She arrived at the concept of
"you-ness," the sum of characteristics that makes somebody special.
This book is a gift to those treasured people.

Marianne continues to create products that help people connect with
those who mean the most to them. Her repertoire includes books,
stationery and giftware.

Marianne shares her unique spirit and enchanting artwork in her other
titles: **The Gift of an Angel, The Gift of a Memory, The Gifts of Being
Grand, I Love You So..., My Shoes Take Me Where I Want to Go,
Dear Daughter, Dear Son, Fish Kisses and Gorilla Hugs,
Dear Granddaughter** and **Dear Grandson.** Plus, she now offers the
Simply Said... and **Smartly Said...** mini book titles for all occasions.

www.mariannerichmond.com.

On the day you were born, the world grew by one

life with big purpose and much to be done.

Look in the mirror. Love who you see.

Stand tall. Smile big. Shout,

"Hooray for Me!"